This is a story of four little Corgis.

Poppy,

Petal,

Pixie,

and Posie,

came home from school,

glowing and rosie.

Mother greeted the pups with a hug.
"I've missed you so much my dear
little loves."

Mother made supper,

while the pups played.

Then they all ate together,
what a wonderful day.

Poppy,

Petal,

Pixie,

and Posie,

lay in their beds,

Said Poppy to Petal, "My blanket's blue!"

Said Pixie to Posie, "My dolly's Roo!"

Mother called up to the pups,
"No more sillies!"

Poppy said, "Please, just a minute...we're all in our beds, just the wrong dog is in it!"

Poppy said, "we know what to do!"

All of the pups did the old
switcheroo!

Poppy, Petal, Pixie and Posie,

back in their beds, comfy cozy.

Four little Corgis say good night to you. What is it time for you to do?

Made in the USA
Columbia, SC
29 July 2017